ISBN: 9781985321168

Author's Note

The Great Depression of the 1930s was a time of extreme hardship for many families. The dust bowl states of Kansas, Oklahoma, Texas, Colorado and New Mexico were especially affected because of drought and falling crop prices. When banks foreclosed, families were forced to leave their homes and migrate to other states looking for work. Unable to provide for their wives and children some men abandoned them. This left women in desperate situations with no home, no money, and children to care for.

The Dime Store Nativity is a work of fiction. It is not based on real events but it could easily have happened. Women, then and now do whatever they must to provide for their children, relying on God to protect them against all odds. I learned about the Faith from my grandmothers, Clorinda Moresi and Katharine Reis, who were themselves mothers during the Great Depression. They did not walk their families alone across the country, but I have no doubt they could have done it if needed. They were wonderful examples of strength and faith in God. This book is dedicated to them and all of the mothers of the 1930s. May their example never be forgotten.

Kathleen Puckett

Illustrator's Note

My father was the age of Eleanor's brother Jacob during the Depression years. Like Jacob, he too had a little red truck with rubber wheels that was given to him one Christmas Eve by The Salvation Army. My father's family did not live in one of the dust bowl states, nor on a farm, nor had to make a journey such as the one Eleanor's family made. They did, however, have to travel from home to home in South Bend, Indiana since they were continually being evicted for lack of rent money. My father's dad had immigrated to the United States from Hungary, and like other men during the 1930s, it was very difficult for him to find work and support his family. The Great Depression and the resulting effects of poverty deeply affected the course of my father's life.

This book is therefore dedicated to my father, John Bencsics, who devoted his life to creating a better world for his family. His determination and perseverance led to a career as a graphic artist and illustrator. After his death in 2014, I ventured into the world of art. As I work, I see him bent over his drawing board, recall his many stories, and am filled with gratitude.

Ellen Bencsics Heitger

This book is a work of fiction.
Any resemblance to people living or
dead is purely coincidental.

Eleanor stood at her living room window looking out at the swirling snow. Christmas lights twinkled on the houses across the street but they did nothing to lessen the sadness surrounding Eleanor's heart. Her husband Everett had died just over a month ago.   After so many years together her heart felt lost without him.

Watching the snow, Eleanor found herself thinking about past Christmases and how happy they had been. The house had always been full of good smells, Christmas decorations, and the sound of loved ones' voices.

Eleanor and Everett had three sons together. The boys would soon be here with their families for Christmas Eve, but Eleanor couldn't seem to find the energy to decorate the house as she usually did.

1

"At least I can put out the nativity," she thought, and turning from the window she went to the oak sideboard to get it. She found the battered red lard tin that it was kept in and set it on the kitchen table.

Taking off the lid she lifted out a piece carefully wrapped in a scrap of flannel. Unwrapping it she found the shepherd carrying a lamb on his shoulder. Next she found Joseph in his green cloak. Then there was one of the wise men kneeling and holding out a gift.

Another wise man followed and then another. At the bottom of the tin she found a donkey, an ox, and baby Jesus in the manger.

Finally she picked up Mary in her blue mantle. It wasn't a fancy set.   It was just a cheap one. The kind that once was sold in dime stores. The years had taken a toll on it.

The blue paint on Mary's gown had faded. One of the legs had been broken off of the lamb. One of the wise men was missing a piece from his crown, but none of that mattered to Eleanor.

This simple little set was something she truly treasured. Just seeing it brought comfort to her. Eleanor sat down at the table and gently picked up Mary.

Her mind drifted back over the years ...

...It was 1935 and Eleanor had just turned 10. After supper one night Mama gathered them all together in the kitchen. Mama sat in her rocking chair with the red tin in her lap.

It was summer, nowhere near Christmas, yet Mama took the lid off and carefully removed each piece. As she set the pieces on the table, she told Eleanor and her little brothers a story .

"Many years ago in a village called Nazareth, there lived a young girl named Mary..."

It was a wonderful story with angels and shepherds and the three wise men who followed a star. Eleanor had always loved the Christmas story but she couldn't understand why Mama was telling it now. It was July and everything was hot and sticky. What was going on?

Then Mama told them a different part of the story. A part Eleanor had never heard before. She told them how an angel appeared to Joseph telling him to move his little family far away to a place called Egypt.

The angel appeared to Joseph and told him that God would protect them on their journey.

But then Mama told them something surprising. They too would be going on a journey, just like Mary and Joseph and the baby Jesus. They were going to walk all the way from where they lived in Oklahoma to where Grandma and Grandpa lived in Iowa.

To the boys, who were only nine and five, the trip sounded like a wonderful adventure. Eleanor, however, was worried. Daddy had been gone for several months. How would he find them if they left the farm?

Mama took Eleanor aside. Tears glistened in her soft blue eyes. Finally she explained that the farm wasn't theirs anymore. It belonged to the bank.

Mama was quiet for a moment and then she said, "Daddy isn't coming back. We'll leave word with the neighbors just in case he does. We have to depend upon the Lord now, Eleanor. Just like Mary and Joseph we will have angels watching over us. There's no need to worry."

Mama sewed burlap knapsacks for herself and the children. They would each be carrying a change of clothes, a cup, a pie plate, a fork, and a spoon. They could also bring one toy.

Eleanor chose her rag doll and Jacob brought his little red truck with the rubber wheels. Elijah had his teddy bear that would ride with him in the red wagon on top of two of Mama's quilts.

When Elijah asked Mama what toy she would be bringing she smiled and said, "There is only one thing I want to bring. I'm taking the nativity set."

They left the next morning after breakfast. The days were hot and dusty as they walked mile after mile. Sometimes a farmer would give them a lift in the back of his truck, but mostly they walked. At night they slept under the stars, lying between Mama's quilts.

Mama had been right. The Lord and His angels did watch over them. Even though there were tough times for everyone, they never went to bed hungry. Whether it was fruit from a tree along the road or eggs and milk from a sympathetic farmwife, they always had something to eat.

Just seeing the red tin riding in the wagon with Elijah filled Eleanor with a sense of security.

It was on a bright day in early September that their little caravan finally arrived at Grandma and Grandpa's farm. Jacob and Elijah ran up ahead, but Eleanor watched in confusion as Mama covered her face and started to cry. She sat down right there in the middle of the dirt road, her shoulders shaking as she cried.

Eleanor watched the boys running to the house. Then suddenly Grandma was there hugging her and thanking Jesus.

Back in her kitchen, Eleanor reflected on the happy years that had followed that arduous journey to Iowa. She had never seen her father again, but the little family had nonetheless been happy on her grandparents' farm. Years later Mama had given her the nativity set as a wedding gift. It remained her most treasured possession.

Thinking about her life, Eleanor realized how blessed she had been. Maybe it was time she shared some of her blessings. She knew just what she had to do.

Getting out some paper Eleanor wrote a letter explaining the story of her nativity set. Next she carefully wrapped each piece and placed them back in the old red tin. Suddenly her heart felt lighter.

Yes, it was time to share her blessings.

Melissa and her children were staying at the women's shelter. She stood by watching them play. What on earth was she going to do? With no job and no place to live Melissa worried constantly about what would happen to them all.

Worst of all, it was almost Christmas Eve. Her eyes filled with tears and she quickly turned away so the children wouldn't see. Everything just seemed so hopeless.

Then Melissa heard a knock on the door of their little room. Sister Anne, who ran the shelter poked her head in.

"Got a minute, Melissa?" she asked.

"Sure Sister," she answered, hoping Sister Anne wouldn't notice the tears she had quickly wiped away.

Sister Anne came in carrying an old and dented red tin in her hands. Smiling she said, "A good friend of mine brought this over asking if there was someone who might need it. You immediately came to mind. There is a letter with it explaining everything."

The nun placed the tin on the bed next to Melissa, handed her the letter, and left as Melissa began to read it.

Her children watched curiously. "What's all this, Mama?" they asked.

Melissa finished reading the letter, smiled and began removing the nativity set from the red tin. As she carefully unwrapped each piece she began to tell them a story...

"Many years ago in a village called Nazareth, there lived a young girl named Mary..."

The meaning of it all filled her with hope and a sudden knowledge that they were not alone. Just like with Eleanor and her family, God was watching over them too.

Things would work out somehow. She suddenly knew it was true. And knowing that was the best Christmas present of all.

Author:

Kathleen Puckett lives in Bristol, Indiana. She is a wife, mother, grandmother, and dedicated elementary school teacher.

Illustrator:

Ellen Bencsics Heitger lives in Mishawaka, Indiana. She is a mother and grandmother. After retiring from teaching, she began a career as an artist. Her days are spent creating art and watching the ducks and geese on the pond behind her studio.

Kathleen and Ellen were teaching in the same elementary school when Kathleen shared a story she had written several years earlier. Having been moved by the story's message, Ellen offered to illustrate it. Thus, began their collaboration and a five-year journey from drafts and sketches to publication.

Made in the USA
Middletown, DE
13 December 2019